Lexi
the Firefly
Fairy

by Daisy Meadows

ORCHARD

The Twilight Fairies' magical powers
Bring harmony to the night-time hours.
But now their magic belongs to me,
And I'll cause chaos, you shall see!

Sunset, moonlight and starlight too,
There'll be no more sweet dreams for you,
From evening dusk to morning light
I am the master of the night!

Contents

A Face in the Bushes

The sun was just setting and the evening starting to grow chilly at Camp Stargaze. Rachel Walker zipped up her fleece and tucked an arm through Kirsty Tate's to keep warm. Rachel and Kirsty were best friends, and their families had come on a camping holiday together for a week.

Exciting things always seemed to happen when the two girls got together — and so far, this holiday was already looking like it would be another very magical one!

Kirsty and Rachel were gathered with about twenty other children at the edge of the campsite. There was going to be a special night-time walk, and everyone was chattering excitedly as they waited to set off.

"Is everyone ready? Then let's go into the Whispering Wood!" called Peter, one of the play-leaders. Kirsty and Rachel walked with the rest of the group into the woodland.

It was cool and dark underneath the leafy trees, and Kirsty flicked on her torch and shone it around. The tall trees swayed in a gentle breeze, and their leaves really did seem to make a whispering sound. "It's creepy being here in the evening, isn't it?" she said to Rachel.

"I know," Rachel replied, glancing into the undergrowth. "Makes you wonder what's in those shadowy corners."

"Whoooo-oooo-oooo!"

Rachel and Kirsty clutched at each other as they heard a ghostly wailing behind them. They spun round to see two boys, Lucas and Matt, laughing so hard they were bent double. "Gotcha!" Matt chortled.

"Your faces! You looked terrified!" Lucas added, his eyes sparkling with mischief.

Kirsty and Rachel laughed too, once their hearts had stopped racing. Those boys! Then Rachel had an idea, and winked at Kirsty. "Oh my goodness!" she said, pretending to gasp in fright. "Look up there – two glowing eyes staring down at us!"

The boys gazed at the tree where Rachel was pointing – and now it was their turn to look scared. "No way!" Matt yelped in alarm. Shining out of the darkness were two gleaming lights, which looked exactly like the eyes of a wild animal. "What is it, do you reckon? A panther?"

"Hmmm," said Kirsty, pretending to think. "It looks like it's a really dangerous...*firefly* or two!" She and Rachel giggled. The glittering lights in the tree were only a couple of flickering fireflies – there was nothing scary or dangerous about them!

Peter, the leader, had overheard. "Wait until we get to the Twinkling Tree," he said. "It always has masses of fireflies around it. It's pretty high up, so the lights of the fireflies can be seen from far away, drawing other fireflies towards it." He grinned. "When they're all twinkling on the branches it's like a Christmas decoration. Or even a magical fairy tree!"

Rachel and Kirsty smiled at one another. They knew all about fairy magic! They were friends with the fairies, and often helped them – especially if horrid Jack Frost and his sneaky goblin servants had been up to their usual tricks!

The group started climbing a hill but Matt stopped walking suddenly. "What was that? I just heard something," he said, shining his torch into the dark undergrowth.

Kirsty rolled her eyes at Rachel. "Not trying to scare us again, are you, Matt?" she said.

Matt shook his head. "No – honestly! I heard a rustling sound in the bushes. Listen!"

The girls stopped and listened. Matt was right – there was a rustling noise nearby. "Do you get bears out here?" Lucas wondered nervously.

15

Peter smiled and shook his head. "No,"
he said. "It's probably just a badger.
Nothing to worry about."

Rachel, Kirsty, Lucas and Matt all shone
their torches into the bushes. Rachel hoped
it was a badger – she'd never seen one
before.

"There – a face!" Lucas cried out,
pointing. He gulped. "I saw a face...but it
was green. What could that be?"

Matt started joking about aliens, but Peter said calmly that it was probably just animals moving the green leaves around, which had only looked like a face. Rachel and Kirsty exchanged a worried look, though. They were pretty sure the green face didn't belong to an alien or an animal, but was something much worse: one of Jack Frost's naughty goblins!

The Twinkling
Tree

"Are you thinking what I'm thinking?"
Rachel asked Kirsty in a low voice.

Kirsty nodded. "Goblins!" she whispered.
"There were goblins about yesterday,
when we helped Ava the Sunset Fairy,
weren't there? There might be more
tonight."

The day before, the girls had met the
seven Twilight Fairies, who looked after
the world between sunset and sunrise —
but all was not well. The Twilight Fairies
had been having a Twilight Party under
the stars when mean

Jack Frost and
his goblins had
stolen their
magic bags
of twilight
dust from
under their
pillows! Since
they'd been without
their magic dust, strange things had been
happening at night, such as the bright
green sunset which had appeared the night
they'd arrived at Camp Stargaze.

"I wonder if we're going to have another fairy adventure tonight," Rachel whispered, her arms prickling with goosebumps. "I hope so!"

"Me too," Kirsty said eagerly. "Let's keep a look-out for anything magical."

The group of campers continued slowly up the hill. "I can't see any fireflies now," Rachel realised, gazing at the dark branches of the trees. "I wonder if they're all in the Twinkling Tree?"

"Probably," Kirsty said. "I can't wait to see it."

After a few more minutes, Peter stopped and spoke to the group. "We should get our first glimpse of the Twinkling Tree soon," he said. He started walking again, still talking. "Once we climb up the last steep bit of the hill, you'll see it shining through the trees. Any minute… Now! Oh." Disappointment filled his voice.

"That's strange," he said. "Where are they?"

Rachel and Kirsty had reached the top of the hill too. They could see a tall, majestic tree through the dusky sky, but its long, leafy branches were empty, without a single firefly to be seen. Peter frowned. "That's a shame," he said. "Usually the Twinkling Tree is a real highlight of this walk. Where can all the fireflies be?"

Kirsty felt disappointed but then Rachel nudged her. "Look," she hissed. "What's that?"

A small spark of light was dancing through the air towards them, and Kirsty peered

through the darkness to make out its shape. Was it a firefly...or could it be a fairy? Somebody else had noticed the moving light too.

"Hey – look!" called Matt excitedly. "There's a firefly. Quick, steer it towards the Twinkling Tree so it can signal to its friends!"

The firefly – if it was a firefly – swerved away abruptly as Lucas and Matt ran towards it. Rachel and Kirsty peered into the darkness, but the light vanished before they could see for sure what it was.

Then Lucas gave a yell. "There's more of them over here!" he shouted, pointing at a cluster of sparkling lights that whizzed and danced through the air in the distance.

The other children rushed to see the sparkles and Kirsty was about to run after them, but Rachel put a hand on her arm. She had just noticed a tiny gleaming figure slip out of the shadows and fly towards them.

"Look!" she hissed excitedly as she recognised the fairy's pretty, smiling face, blonde wavy hair held back in a green band, and a twinkling silver sequinned miniskirt, with baseball boots to match. It was Lexi the Firefly Fairy!

"Hello again," Kirsty said in delight, holding her jacket pocket wide open so that Lexi could dive into it and hide.

"Phew!" said Lexi. "That was close – I thought those boys had spotted me. I had to conjure up some flying sparkles in the nick of time!"

Kirsty and Rachel moved out of sight, behind the low-hanging branches of the Twilight Tree. "Good thinking," Rachel grinned. "It's nice to see you again, Lexi. We were wondering what had happened to the fireflies that usually gather here. Do you know?"

"I do," Lexi said. "It's all because of Jack Frost. He knows how important the fireflies are. Not only do they make summer nights special in the human world with their lovely flickering lights, but they also provide light to the Fairyland Palace, and the fairies' toadstool houses, too. Usually, I have my magic bag of fire dust which keeps the fireflies lit up. But since Jack Frost and his goblins stole my dust, the fireflies' lights have gone out – and Fairyland is in darkness!"

"Oh no," Kirsty said. "Can we help look for your bag of fire dust? We helped Ava find her sunbeam dust yesterday."

"I heard," Lexi said. "That's really good news! And yes please, I'd love you to help me too. Would you mind coming to Fairyland with me?"

"Mind?" Rachel echoed. "We'd love to!" She and Kirsty knew that they were quite safe to leave the other children as time always stood still while they were in Fairyland. They would be able to fly off and have an exciting adventure, and nobody in the human world would notice they'd gone!

"Fantastic," Lexi replied. "First, let me turn you into fairies..." She waved her wand over the two girls and they felt their bodies shrink smaller and smaller, until they were the same size as Lexi. Both girls had glittering fairy wings on their backs and they fluttered them in delight.

"Now let's go to Fairyland!" Lexi cried, throwing more fairy dust over the three of them.

A sparkling whirlwind spun around, and Kirsty and Rachel were whirled up into the air. Another fairy adventure was beginning!

Fairyland in Darkness

After several moments, Rachel and Kirsty felt themselves gently landing again. The glittering whirlwind cleared…and both girls blinked in surprise. Usually when they came to Fairyland, it was light and sunny there, with sweet little toadstool houses and flowers everywhere, and the beautiful Fairyland Palace gleaming on the hillside.

Tonight, however, most of Fairyland was pitch black, and it took a moment for the girls' and Lexi's eyes to adjust to the darkness.

"Wow," Rachel said, peering into the gloom. "Where are we? I can hardly see a thing!"

The end of Lexi's wand was sparkling and she held it up in front of them like a torch. They could just see the vague outline of a toadstool house in front of them, with its sloping roof and little wooden door. "I think this is where Summer the Holiday Fairy lives," Lexi replied –

and at that moment, the door of the house opened, and out came Summer herself.

"Lexi, is that you?" she asked, shivering. "Flicker's light won't go on."

"Where are you, Flicker?" Lexi called. "Are you there?"

From out of the darkness came the sound of beating wings, and then an insect flew over and landed on Lexi's palm. Neither Rachel nor Kirsty had ever seen a firefly close up before, and they gazed in interest at Flicker's sleek black and gold shell.

He was about the size that a robin would be to them in the human world, and his expression was sad.

"I usually sit on Summer's windowsill in the evenings to give her light," Flicker explained. "Then, once she's gone to bed, I fly to the stream with my friend Glimmer. There's a night rose that grows there, and the nectar is delicious." His antennae drooped miserably. "But without my light, Glimmer won't be able to find me. And neither of us will be able to find the rose!"

"Oh dear," Lexi said, stroking Flicker's back. "I'm sorry to hear that. We're

searching for my magic bag of fire dust
and as soon as we find it, I'll be able
to turn all the
fireflies' lights on
again, but until
then—"

Lexi stopped
talking, her face
alert. Kirsty
and Rachel
became aware
of a commotion nearby, and listened.
They could hear voices – loud, and
argumentative, coming nearer by the
second.

"You've got it all wrong!" the first voice
grumbled. "I've caught four, and you've
caught two. It's no good pretending you
got the last one, because you didn't."

"I totally did! You're making things up!" the second one shouted. "You're just jealous because I'm better at catching them than you!"

Kirsty and Rachel shrank into the shadows as the voices came nearer still. They would know those bad-tempered, harsh-sounding voices anywhere – they belonged to the goblins!

"What are they up to, I wonder?" Summer whispered, as they stood huddled in her doorway.

They didn't have to wait long to find
out. The goblins suddenly came into view,
and the four friends saw that they were
carrying torches, which cast golden beams
through the darkness. They also held what
looked like lanterns, but there was no light
coming from them.

When the goblins spotted the fairies
gathered outside Summer's house with
Flicker on Lexi's palm, they
looked delighted. "Aha!
There's another!" the
tallest goblin shouted
and then, before the
fairies could stop
him, he snatched
Flicker, shoved him
into a lantern…and
ran off!

"Hey!" shouted Lexi, but it was too late. The goblins had vanished into the distance. The four fairies could now see other shadowy figures running around, all with lanterns. From the goblins' shouts of glee, it was clear that they were stealing every firefly they could find.

"What are they doing? Why are they taking the fireflies?" Rachel asked, bewildered.

"I don't know," Lexi said grimly, "but I bet it's got something to do with Jack Frost, and my fire dust! I'm going to follow them, and see what's happening."

"We'll come with you," Kirsty offered at once.

"And I'll warn the other fairies what the goblins are up to," Summer vowed.

"Thanks, Summer," said Lexi, then she turned to Kirsty and Rachel. "Come on – there's no time to lose!

Follow Those Goblins!

Kirsty, Rachel and Lexi set off through the darkness. It was easy to follow the goblins, because they were so noisy, and also because they had their torches, which lit the way. The three friends hung back in the shadows so as not to be spotted.

After a few minutes on the goblins' trail, Lexi's eyes narrowed. "They're going to Jack Frost's Ice Castle," she whispered.

"What *is* he plotting, I wonder?"

As they rounded a corner, the three fairies gasped in disbelief. Jack Frost's castle was usually a grim, forbidding place with its icy walls and patrolling guards, but this evening, it looked positively cheery and welcoming, lit up as it was against the dark sky. "Wow!" Kirsty breathed. "I've never seen it so beautiful."

"Yes," Lexi said, sounding cross. "And it's only beautiful because he's used

my special fire dust to light up all the fireflies he's got trapped in lanterns, look!" As Rachel and Kirsty flew across the moat, closer to the castle, they realised that Lexi was right. Glowing lanterns hung in every window, and inside each lantern flickered a firefly. "How selfish!" Rachel fumed. "Stealing all the fireflies and trapping them, just so that his castle can be lit up!"

"I know," Lexi said. "The poor things. They aren't as bright as they usually are – they must be feeling very sad."

"Look, there's Jack Frost," Kirsty hissed, seeing the spiky, cold figure appearing in his doorway. "Hide!"

The three fairies hid inside a bush, and Lexi muttered some magic words which made the light of her wand go out. They

peered through the leaves to see Jack Frost
holding a small bag which cast a magical
glow into the murky waters of his moat.
As the goblins trooped into the castle with
their lanterns full of fireflies, Jack Frost
sprinkled fire dust on each firefly, making
them light up. "Now it won't be dark any
more," Jack Frost said
gleefully, a smug
smile on his face.

"They've
caught so many,"
Rachel said.
"I bet it was a
goblin Lucas saw in
the Whispering Wood. Jack Frost
must have sent the goblins into the human
world to steal fireflies there, as well as
Fairyland!"

"We've got to rescue the fireflies," Lexi said. "We can't leave them trapped in lanterns, as Jack Frost's prisoners. They should be free to fly around wherever they please!"

Kirsty and Rachel agreed. But how could they release the fireflies when they were right under Jack Frost's nose?

"We'd be able to sneak into the castle if it was dark," Kirsty said, "but we can't chance it now, with the fireflies' lights flashing on and off. We'd be seen straightaway."

Rachel thought. "Is there a way to tell the fireflies to turn their lights off?" she wondered. "That would make everything dark again."

Lexi nodded. "I could use my wand to show them," she replied, sounding more cheerful. "Let's see if this works."

She fluttered above the bushes and muttered some magic words which made the tip of her wand sparkle and shine through the dark sky.

Then, with another magical command, she turned the wand's light off.

Lexi, Kirsty and Rachel held their breath as they stared at the fireflies. Had they seen Lexi's light? Had they understood the message?

Some of the fireflies' lights vanished, making the castle slightly darker, but most of the lanterns remained lit up.

"I'll try again," Lexi said, turning the light of her wand on again, and then off. This time, more of the fireflies seemed to have seen her light, and understood the message. Lots of their little lights turned to black and the castle became much darker.

"It's working," Kirsty said excitedly. "Clever fireflies!"

Lexi turned her wand on, then off one more time, and the last remaining fireflies turned their lights off too – plunging Jack Frost's castle into total darkness.

"What's going on? Turn those lights back on!" the girls heard Jack Frost splutter. Then they heard his footsteps hurrying into the castle, and heard him shouting frantically to his servants.

"Now's our chance, come on!" Lexi hissed, and she, Kirsty and Rachel tiptoed towards the castle. Rachel hardly dared breathe as they crept silently up to the doorway.

Would Jack Frost see them? And what would he do to them if he did?

Glow, Glow, Glow!

Rachel, Kirsty and Lexi pressed close to the walls as they sneaked through the open doors of Jack Frost's Ice Castle. They could hear his booming voice from further within the castle ordering the lights to be put on, but managed to escape down one of the corridors without anyone noticing them.

The three friends flew silently along the corridor, their eyes straining to see through the darkness. They fluttered into every room they could find, opening the lanterns and setting the fireflies free.

"Quick, back to the fairy houses, you'll be safer there," Lexi whispered to the fireflies.

It was tricky, trying to work quickly in the darkness – and nerve-racking too, when they could hear Jack Frost bellowing in the background. "What's wrong with this fire dust? Why have the fireflies stopped shining? I don't want it to be dark!" he yelled.

"Hurry, hurry," Lexi urged Kirsty and Rachel. "We've got to be as fast as we can!"

As the fireflies flew out of the castle windows, they turned on their flickering lights once more. It was lovely to see them whizz through the darkness like tiny shooting stars, twinkling in the night sky, one after another.

On and on the fairies flew, from room to room, releasing the fireflies. The goblins had obviously told Jack Frost that the fireflies were escaping because the three friends heard him shout with rage, ordering his goblins to chase after the fireflies and catch them again. "I will not put up with this darkness!" he thundered.

"He's so silly!" Lexi sighed. "The fireflies are so friendly they would happily light up his castle if he just asked them. Why did he have to try to trap them? They'll stay well away from him now."

"At least they can still glow from the magic dust Jack Frost sprinkled on them," Rachel pointed out, opening another lantern and setting free the firefly inside it. "They can fly back to the toadstool houses now – and hopefully the Twinkling Tree too."

"Yes," Lexi agreed, "but the fire dust on them won't last forever, unfortunately." She opened another lantern to let out the firefly, and watched as it flew away. They were right at the very top of Jack Frost's castle now, and the firefly soared into the air, its light gleaming. "There," she said. "That's the last one. The fireflies are all free!" She put her hands on her hips. "Now we just need to get my bag of fire dust off Jack Frost and we can get out of here."

Kirsty swallowed nervously.

"How are we going to do that?" she wondered aloud. Sneaking into the

Ice Castle and setting the fireflies free had
been scary enough, but the thought of
trying to get Lexi's bag of fire dust from
Jack Frost was even scarier!

There was silence while they all thought.
It was hard to concentrate, though, when
they could still
hear Jack Frost
shouting at his
goblins. "I need
those fireflies
back NOW!" he
bawled.

His words gave
Rachel an idea. "Jack
Frost really wants the fireflies... so maybe
we could somehow trick him into thinking
we're fireflies," she suggested.

"Yes! If you could use your magic, Lexi,

to make us look like fireflies, it'll mean we can get close to him — close enough to grab the bag of fire dust!" Kirsty added.

"That's a great idea," Lexi said, waving her wand in a complicated pattern. Streams of bright magic spiralled from the end of it, swirling all around.

Seconds later, Kirsty and Rachel felt themselves shrinking smaller and smaller, until Lexi seemed like a giant next to them. "Now to make you glow, glow, glow!" Lexi smiled, waving her wand again.

Rachel giggled as she felt a fizzing sensation all over – and looked down at herself to see that her legs and feet were shining brightly. "Cool!" she laughed.

The three of them flew out of the window, Kirsty and Rachel gleaming in the darkness just like two little fireflies. They swooped low over the goblins who were gathered outside with Jack Frost. Jack Frost saw them and gave a shout. "There are two more! Catch them!"

Rachel and Kirsty zipped

away in different directions with goblins chasing after each of them. Rachel flew in loop-the-loops, while Kirsty flew in a zigzag pattern, making the goblins puff and pant to keep up.

Rachel was getting rather dizzy with all her looping, and decided to zoom straight ahead, the goblins still chasing her. But Kirsty had had the same idea, and was also whizzing along in a straight line – and she was headed straight for Rachel!

"Watch out!" Lexi called in alarm. "You're going to crash!"

Firefly Magic

At the very last moment, Rachel swerved out of the way of Kirsty, and Kirsty managed to zip up high in the air. But the goblins who'd been chasing after them weren't quite so nimble — and ended up crashing into each other, and knocking over Jack Frost!

Just then, the moon slid out from behind
a cloud, casting a silvery light over the
grounds of the castle. Rachel saw to
her excitement that Jack Frost had three
or four goblins piled on top of him and
couldn't move. Even better, she
could see Lexi's bag of fire
dust sticking out of his
pocket!

She darted
down, her heart
thumping, and
just managed
to pull out
the bag of
dust and fly
into the air
with it.

It was

rather heavy, but luckily, Lexi had seen
her, and quickly waved her wand to make
the bag light enough for Rachel to carry.

Then Lexi soared over to Rachel, and
took the bag gratefully from her. "Well
done!" she exclaimed. "Come
on, let's get out of here
before they untangle
themselves!"

The three
friends flew over
the moat and
landed briefly
so that Lexi
could turn
Kirsty and
Rachel
back into
fairies.

They were just about to set off again,
when Lexi noticed a group of fireflies,
including Flicker, on a thorny bush.
Strange! Why hadn't they flown off with
the others?

"Are you all right?" she asked the
fireflies.

"We're fine," Flicker replied, wiggling
her antennae happily. "In fact, we're more
than fine. We've found a lovely patch

of night rose plants here with plenty of delicious nectar, so we're going to make a new home here together."

"Oh, OK," Lexi replied. She smiled at Kirsty and Rachel. "At least Jack Frost and the goblins will have some light now, I suppose."

Once they were back in the Fairyland village, Lexi gathered all the fireflies that had come from the human world and waved her wand, sending them back to the Whispering Wood, together with Kirsty and Rachel.

As the sparkly whirlwind vanished, Kirsty and Rachel found themselves still fairy-sized, and right at the top of the Twinkling Tree, along with hundreds of flickering fireflies!

"Wow!" cried the children below, gazing up at the tree which was now twinkling and sparkling all over, thanks to the fireflies' lights.

"They're back!" Peter shouted in delight. "There – doesn't it look amazing?"

Up in the tree, Lexi hugged Kirsty and Rachel goodbye. "Thanks for everything," she said. "Now I'd better turn you back into your usual size, so you can see how pretty the tree looks from the ground too!"

With a last wave of Lexi's wand, Kirsty and Rachel felt their bodies tingle with fairy magic... and seconds later, found themselves at the back of the group, gazing up at the Twinkling Tree.

"Oh, wow," Rachel sighed. "It's beautiful!"

"The fireflies look like fairies," said a little girl nearby, and Rachel and Kirsty turned to grin at one another.

If only the girl knew that they had been fairies up there in the tree just seconds earlier!

"That was really exciting," Kirsty said happily. "Definitely the most de-light-ful adventure yet!"

Now Kirsty and Rachel
must help...

Zara the Starlight Fairy

Read on for a sneak peek...

"This telescope is huge, Kirsty!" Rachel Walker said excitedly to her best friend, Kirsty Tate. "I can't wait to have a look at the night sky."

"It's going to be amazing," Kirsty agreed as they stared up at the enormous silver telescope.

The girls were spending a week of the summer holidays with their parents at Camp Stargaze, which had its very own observatory for studying the stars. The observatory was a square white building topped with a large dome, and charts and pictures of the night sky hung on the walls.

In the middle of the observatory stood the gigantic telescope, and Professor Hetty, the camp astronomer, was explaining to Rachel, Kirsty and the other children about the stars and constellations.

"As you know, this area was chosen for Camp Stargaze because we can get really clear views of the night sky from here," Professor Hetty reminded them. She was a jolly, round-faced woman with twinkling blue eyes and a mop of red hair.

"Have any of you ever done a join-the-dots puzzle?"

All the children looked puzzled, but everyone nodded.

"Well, a constellation is rather like a join-the-dots puzzle!" Professor Hetty explained with a smile. "A constellation is made of individual stars that join up to make a picture, just like the puzzle. But although the stars look close together to us here on earth, sometimes they're actually millions of miles apart! Let's take a look, shall we?"

Professor Hetty pressed a button on the wall. There was a noise overhead, and Rachel and Kirsty glanced up to see a large section of the domed roof slide smoothly back, revealing the dark, velvety night sky and the sparkling silver stars twinkling here and there like diamonds in a jewellery box. Everyone gasped and applauded.

"Wonderful!" Professor Hetty said eagerly. "I never get tired of looking at the night sky. It's so magical."

Rachel nudged Kirsty. "Professor Hetty doesn't know just how magical the night-time really is!" she whispered.

Kirsty smiled. When she and Rachel had arrived at Camp Stargaze, Ava the Sunset Fairy had rushed from Fairyland to ask for their help. The girls had discovered that Ava and the other six Twilight Fairies made sure the hours from dusk to dawn were peaceful and well-ordered, with the help of their satin bags of magical fairy dust.

But while the Twilight Fairies were enjoying a party under the stars with their fairy friends, Jack Frost had broken into the Fairyland Palace with his naughty goblin servants. The goblins had stolen the magical bags that were hidden under the Twilight Fairies' pillows. Then, with a wave of his ice wand, Jack Frost had sent the goblins and the bags spinning away to hide in the human world. Jack Frost's plan was to cause night-time chaos for both fairies and humans, but Rachel, Kirsty and the Twilight Fairies were determined not to let that happen.

"I wonder if we'll meet another Twilight Fairy today?" Kirsty murmured to Rachel as they all lined up to have a look through the telescope. "I'm so glad we managed to find Ava's and Lexi's magical bags, but we still have five more to go!"

Read Zara the Starlight Fairy to find out what adventures are in store for Kirsty and Rachel!

Meet the
Twilight Fairies

Kirsty and Rachel must rescue the Twilight Fairies' magical bags from Jack Frost or nobody will ever enjoy a night's rest again!

www.rainbowmagicbooks.co.uk

RAINBOW magic®

Meet the fairies, play games
and get sneak peeks at
the latest books!

There's fairy fun for everyone at

www.rainbowmagicbooks.co.uk

You'll find great activities, competitions, stories and
fairy profiles, and also a special newsletter.

Win Rainbow Magic Goodies!

There are lots of Rainbow Magic fairies, and we want to know which one is your favourite! Send us a picture of her and tell us in thirty words why she is your favourite and why you like Rainbow Magic books. Each month we will put the entries into a draw and select one winner to receive a Rainbow Magic Sparkly T-shirt and Goody Bag!

Send your entry on a postcard to Rainbow Magic Competition, Orchard Books, 338 Euston Road, London NW1 3BH.
Australian readers should email: childrens.books@hachette.com.au
New Zealand readers should write to Rainbow Magic Competition, PO Box 3255, Shortland St, Auckland 1140, NZ.
Don't forget to include your name and address.
Only one entry per child.

Good luck!

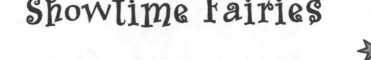

Meet the Showtime Fairies

Madison the Magic Show Fairy

Leah the Theatre Fairy

Alesha the Acrobat Fairy

Darcey the Dance Diva Fairy

Taylor the Talent Show Fairy

Amelia the Singing Fairy

Isla the Ice Star Fairy

Collect them all to find out how Kirsty and Rachel help their magical friends to save the Tippington Variety Show!

www.rainbowmagicbooks.co.uk